SUPERNATURAL
THE TELEVISION SERIES

Your Guide to
Spirit Boards

Noetta Harjo

T0364048

CONTENTS

Introduction

A good hunter knows the ins and outs of the spirit world. They also know the dangers of the supernatural and how to navigate this realm cautiously. Good hunters know how to summon spirits and which tools to use if the entities become hostile. That's why the Mini Spirit Board is a must-have for the serious supernatural hunter. Spirits are everywhere, whether you see them or not, and the Mini Spirit Board helps a hunter communicate with the dead to make sure they are benign, to find out where an object is hidden, or to help a friendly ghost with unfinished business.

Some of the spirits hunters may encounter don't even know they are dead, while others simply refuse to leave. Those who stay can become bothersome. Sometimes they're merely mischievous and sometimes they turn violent. Some spirits linger so long, they become complacent with their situation. Whatever the case, spirits are a part of our world, and they have a lot to say.

Spirit Boards in *Supernatural* and Beyond

Supernatural aired for fifteen seasons, during which Sam and Dean Winchester experienced many encounters with spirits. Over the course of their adventures, the hunters often sought out ghosts, demons, vampires, werewolves, and other supernatural beings. Other times, the Winchesters were the ones being hunted. Their parents had also been hunters and equipped the boys with the necessary skills to stay safe while hunting, and oftentimes that means finding ways to interact with spirits.

Communicating with the dead is an age-old fascination for humankind. Many people assert that you must truly believe in ghosts for the board to work. There are even common misconceptions, like that the board invites unwanted possession or the conjuring of a demonic presence. For others, a spirit board is merely a game.

In the world of *Supernatural*, Sam and Dean have proven the existence of spirits and the effectiveness of the spirit board. It is a serious tool for hunters and has saved the Winchesters' lives once or twice. You too can use the Mini Spirit Board to communicate with the great beyond.

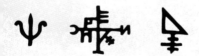

How to Use a Spirit Board

Although the spirit board's origin is never discussed onscreen, it is an easily recognized object. The device is a flat board with letters and numbers printed on top, along with the words "Yes," "No," and "Goodbye." The living user or users ask a question, either to a specific spirit or to any spirit who may be in the room.

The spirit guides the users' hands to move a planchette, a teardrop-shaped tool that indicates the answers. The spirit can spell out words to give the living user more specific answers to their questions, or they can simply use *yes* or *no*. The spirit can also move the plank to *goodbye* for an exit out of the conversation.

There have been many uses for the spirit board on *Supernatural*. It's been used to connect with dead (and sometimes, as in the case of Dean's coma in season 2, semi-dead) spirits, to locate supernatural objects and people, and even to kill. The board may not always work. Sometimes the spirits aren't near enough, and sometimes they just don't want to answer. It's important to have respect for their power. Beware of those who abuse the spirit board for a quick buck. And always end the conversation when you receive a *goodbye*.

The spirit board was first used by Sam Winchester in season 2, episode 1, "In My Time of Dying." The boys and their father, John Winchester, were in a terrible car accident that left Dean in a coma. Though Dean was not dead, his spirit lingered in the hospital. Sam sensed Dean's presence while sitting next to his hospital bed. He used a spirit board to talk to his brother. Sam calls the device a "talking board." And despite Dean's skepticism, the talking board worked!

Dean was not the only spirit inhabiting the hospital. A reaper roamed the halls to collect the souls of the deceased patients, and that reaper decided Dean's time on Earth was up. Through the spirit board, Dean was able to tell Sam about the Reaper. Dean was saved after Papa Winchester made a deal with a demon for Dean's life. The demon stopped the Reaper from taking Dean's soul, and Dean woke up. This would be the only time Dean put his hands on a spirit board in the entire series.

Associates and adversaries of the Winchesters also used spirit boards to connect with the dead. In season 3, episode 3, "Bad Day at Black Rock," the boys met a brilliant thief named Bela Talbot. Bela was hired to find a cursed rabbit's foot that gave the owner great luck. But if the owner ever lost the rabbit's foot, they would die in a most unfortunate way. Bela used the spirit board to ask those unlucky deceased individuals where she could find the cursed rabbit's foot. It turned out it was located in

John Winchester's storage unit. Sam became the temporary owner of the rabbit's foot before losing it to Bela, and then Dean tracked her down to take the cursed rabbit's foot back so they could destroy it before Sam was killed. They were successful in the destruction of the rabbit's foot, but the spirit board was damaged in the process. Bela shot at Dean and hit the board instead.

Bela Talbot returned that same season in episode 7, "Fresh Blood." A hunter named Gordon Walker was hunting the Winchesters. He knew of Bela's recent run-in with the brothers and bargained for their location. When Dean found out that Bela betrayed them, he vowed to kill her.

Bela did not like people holding grudges against her. So she used a spirit board to find Gordon. She called Dean to make amends and to pass along Gordon's whereabouts. The spirits also sent a message to Dean: Bela said they told Dean to run, leave town, and not go after Gordon. Dean did not listen to the spirits and was almost killed by a vampire. The lesson here is to listen to the spirits when they warn you about impending doom.

And yet people in the world of the show are still skeptical about spirit boards, probably because some so-called psychics use the board to con people out of their money. We met such a charlatan in season 7, episode 7, "The Mentalists." A medium used a spirit board and a lot of parlor tricks to make her customers believe a spirit was among them. A spirit did in fact show up, but not the spirit the couple wanted to talk to. This particular spirit was hostile and used the planchette to kill the medium. Perhaps the spirit was angered by the medium's deception.

Sam and Dean investigated multiple murders of mediums in the most psychic town in America, Lily Dale, and while the mediums might not have been the real deal, a real psychic *was* responsible for the murders. He was controlling a spirit and using it to kill the competition.

Sometimes the spirit board doesn't work. This may be because there are no spirits nearby, the spirits do not want to communicate, or something is suppressing the lines of communication. The latter occurred in season 7, episode 19, "Of Grave Importance." This was a dark time in *Supernatural* history. Family friend and father figure Bobby Singer had just died, but his spirit hung around for a little while. During that time, Bobby tried communicating with the boys, but they never caught on.

Bobby's spirit was attached to his flask. Dean carried that flask with him everywhere after Bobby died, so Bobby was always with him.

In this episode, a friend of Bobby's died in a haunted house and her spirit was trapped. When Bobby learned how to move objects, he was able to communicate with Dean by steaming up the bathroom mirror, and Sam and Dean managed to release Bobby's friend from her imprisonment. They also got a chance to finally see and talk to Bobby.

The encounter was emotional because Sam had previously tried several times to use his talking board to reach Bobby. One night, when the boys were sharing a beer, Dean had picked up his beer and found it empty. Sam had thought maybe Bobby's spirit was in the room, so he'd used the talking board. But Bobby had never answered because he was always with Dean. After they finally did encounter him, Bobby was more visible to the brothers until he eventually moved on to another plane of existence.

Conclusion

There is no scientific evidence that spirit boards actually work, but science can't explain everything. All we can do is experience the board for ourselves to find out.

The talking board is a staple in occult studies. Even if ghosts aren't your specialty, hunters can still benefit from using the spirit board to find the items or beings they are looking for.

Whatever your needs, be respectful and take the experience seriously. Start your journey to becoming a great hunter with the Mini Spirit Board. The key is to believe.

This book has been bound using handcraft methods and Smyth-sewn to ensure durability.

Designed by
Tanvi Baghele.